YEARBOOK

by Tracey West
Grosset & Dunlap
An Imprint of Penguin Group (USA) Inc.

GROSSET & DUNLAP
Published by the Penguin Group
Penguin Group (USA) Inc., 375 Hudson Street, New York,
New York 10014, USA
Penguin Group (Canada), 90 Eglinton Avenue East, Suite 700,
Toronto, Ontario M4P 2Y3, Canada
(a division of Pearson Penguin Canada Inc.)
Penguin Books Ltd., 80 Strand, London WC2R 0RL, England
Penguin Group Ireland, 25 St. Stephen's Green, Dublin 2, Ireland
(a division of Penguin Books Ltd.)
Penguin Group (Australia), 250 Camberwell Road,
Camberwell, Victoria 3124, Australia
(a division of Pearson Australia Group Pty. Ltd.)
Penguin Books India Pvt. Ltd., 11 Community Centre, Panchsheel Park,
New Delhi—110 017, India
Penguin Group (NZ), 67 Apollo Drive, Rosedale, Auckland 0632, New Zealand
(a division of Pearson New Zealand Ltd.)
Penguin Books (South Africa) (Pty.) Ltd., 24 Sturdee Avenue,
Rosebank, Johannesburg 2196, South Africa

Penguin Books Ltd., Registered Offices:
80 Strand, London WC2R 0RL, England

Published by Grosset & Dunlap, a division of Penguin Young Readers Group,
345 Hudson Street, New York, New York 10014. GROSSET & DUNLAP
is a trademark of Penguin Group (USA) Inc. Manufactured in China.

ISBN 978-0-448-45755-0   10 9 8 7 6 5 4 3 2 1

Table of Contents

Let the Puppy Bowl Begin!

Every year since 2005, fans around the globe have gathered in front of their television sets, their tails wagging with excitement—but not for the big game. Instead, they tune in to Animal Planet™, eager to watch the most spectacular canine competition on air: the Puppy Bowl!

For two hours, a stellar lineup of the country's most adorable puppies frolic, tumble, and race around a puppy-sized football field. The Ref keeps score. Hamsters keep watch from a blimp in the sky. Chicken cheerleaders cluck from the sidelines. And supercute kittens perform in an unforgettable halftime show.

Now you can hold your favorite memories of every Puppy Bowl right in your own hands! On the pages of this book, you'll find photos and information on the team from Puppy Bowl VII, plus highlights from all seven games. We've made sure to include everything that fans love about the Puppy Bowl—kittens, hamsters, chickens, bunnies, tail-gaters, and even an interview with the lovable Ref.

So if you think you can't make it until the next Puppy Bowl, don't despair. There is enough mutt mayhem in this book to last you until the next one, we promise!

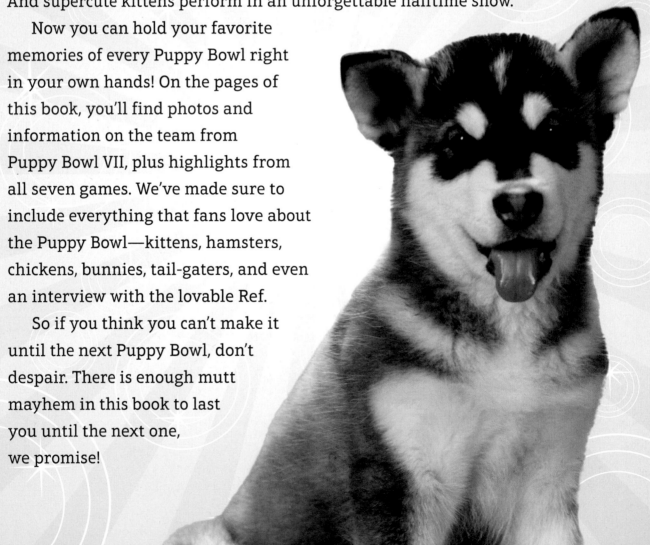

Puppy Bowl VII Team Roster

What does it take to earn a spot in the starting lineup for Puppy Bowl? Animal Planet™ puts the call out to many trusted dog rescue agencies each year to find puppies that fit the bill. The puppies they choose have to be in good health and get along with other dogs. And, of course, they've got to be cute—but what puppy isn't?

For Puppy Bowl VII, the dogs were the usual mix of sweet mutts, tiny toy dogs, athletic sporting dogs, energetic terriers, and everything in between. Which one is your favorite?

AMY

Breed(s): golden retriever/corgi mix
Age: 18 weeks
Fun Fact: loves a good facial

Amy may look like a sweet puffball, but her powerful moves are solid gold. Amy is an interesting mix of breeds. Golden retrievers are big and outgoing, while corgis are small and tough.

BIG RED

Breed(s): shepherd mix
Age: 13 weeks
Fun Fact: loves classic TV shows

When the whistle blew, Big Red was ready to tear things up on the field. In the final quarter of the game, River, the Great Pyrenees, stole the ball from him, but Big Red snatched it back in a dramatic play.

BOODA

Breed(s): pug mix
Age: 15 weeks
Fun Fact: meditates regularly

Despite his peaceful nature, this pup likes to ruff it up now and then. The fans enjoyed watching this cute, little guy getting frisky on the field.

BROWNIE SUNDAE

Breed(s): cocker spaniel mix
Age: 10 weeks
Fun Fact: spelling bee champion

Brownie Sundae turned out to be a sweet teammate when she partnered up with Mae to develop a secret scoring strategy. But later in the game, she was called out for Unnecessary Ruff-Ruff-Ruffness. Maybe she's not so sweet after all?

CALVIN

Breed(s): border terrier mix
Age: 15 weeks
Fun Fact: is a member of a book club

This little guy is one real hot dog of a hound. He put on a great show on the field, barking and getting possession of the ball multiple times. In a dramatic moment in the first quarter, he took the ball all the way to the end zone—and stopped paws short of making a touchdown!

CB

Breed(s): shih tzu/beagle mix
Age: 16 weeks
Fun Fact: loves the Sunday crossword puzzle

As soon as the game began, CB became a fast, furry blur on the field as he raced up and down it. CB and Calvin quickly bonded. Sometimes they worked together, and other times CB tried to swipe the ball from his new friend.

CHARLIE

Breed(s): Yorkshire terrier mix
Age: 14 weeks
Fun Fact: prefers the bedhead look

Charlie is one tough ball of fluff! He probably gets this from the Yorkie in him. These small dogs are known to be brave and even bossy at times. They've also got lots of energy, which is a great quality for a Puppy Bowl player.

CHIH

Breed(s): shih tzu
Age: 11 weeks
Fun Fact: has a twin brother

Thoughtful Chih is a calming force on the field. But that doesn't mean that he was afraid of getting into the action every now and again, even if his twin brother, Shang, was the more aggressive of the two.

DUNCAN

Breed(s): golden retriever/
bulldog mix
Age: 16 weeks
Fun Fact: kitten bodyguard

This cute canine was very curious on the field. Duncan spent a lot of time sniffing out his opponents. Was he just being friendly or working on a strategy? We may never know.

JACK

Breed(s): lab mix
Age: 12 weeks
Fun Fact: deals cards at a casino

This high-energy pup made a name for himself on the field, stealing the ball whenever he could and pouncing on players whenever he got a chance. In the second quarter, he took things too far and got called out for Unnecessary Ruff-Ruff-Ruffness.

JESSIE

Breed(s): shepherd mix
Age: 13 weeks
Fun Fact: is a double Dutch champion

Jessie had a great run in the second quarter, charging across the field into the end zone. But she stopped just short of the goal line. This pup was too pooped to score!

KODA

Breed(s): Siberian husky
Age: 16 weeks
Fun Fact: favorite holiday is Columbus Day

Siberian huskies are born team players. On the field, Koda bonded with Max. The spunky pup was half Koda's size, but Koda treated his teammate with respect.

LINDY

Breed(s): Brittany spaniel/schnauzer mix
Age: 14 weeks
Fun Fact: travels in a private jet

Brittany spaniels are good hunting dogs. That's probably why Lindy can use her nose to sniff out her opponents' fear. She's also part schnauzer, which means she has a lot of energy.

LITTLE RED

Breed(s): shih tzu/beagle mix
Age: 16 weeks
Fun Fact: has a culinary degree

He may be small in size, but he's big in attitude. During the game, he wasn't afraid to take on border terrier Calvin—and got nipped in the back end for his troubles.

LOUISE

Breed(s): rat terrier/lab/hound mix
Age: 11 weeks
Fun Fact: speaks three languages

Some people say that rat terriers make good watchdogs. Maybe that's why Louise is such a great defensive player. With Louise on guard, good luck getting to the goal!

MADDIE

Breed(s): Yorkshire terrier mix
Age: 9 weeks
Fun Fact: owns a pottery wheel

This pup is so small and fluffy that it was hard to tell her apart from the fuzzy footballs on the field! Luckily, none of the other players tried to run her in for a touchdown.

MAE

Breed(s): Great Pyrenees/ Newfoundland mix
Age: 9 weeks
Fun Fact: collects designer purses

Great Pyrenees and Newfoundlands are large dogs that are considered to be "giant" breeds. When Mae grows up, she'll be a force to be reckoned with, but right now it's her big heart that makes her a champion.

MAX

Breed(s): lab/spaniel mix
Age: 10 weeks
Fun Fact: loves show tunes

Max may not have made any big plays in the game, but with a face like that, who really cares? Any coach would be proud to have this adorable puppy on his team.

MOLLY

Breed(s): boxer mix
Age: 11 weeks
Fun Fact: plays the harmonica

People say that boxers are playful and athletic—two good qualities for any Puppy Bowl player. Guess that makes Molly a perfect team member!

OLIVER

Breed(s): Great Pyrenees
Age: 9 weeks
Fun Fact: is a movie buff

Great Pyrenees dogs are known to be very independent, but Oliver made a good team on the field with his brother River. The two boys bulldozed the other players as they charged across the field.

PATCH

Breed(s): cocker spaniel mix
Age: 10 weeks
Fun Fact: attends the opera regularly

This pup entered the field with his game face on. But cocker spaniels really enjoy being at home with their families, so a full-time football career is probably out of the question for Patch.

PAULY

Breed(s): smooth fox terrier
Age: 14 weeks
Fun Fact: spins records as a DJ

In the third quarter, things really heated up when Shang stole the ball from Pauly. Shang's brother Chih got involved, and the puppies tangled for control of the ball. In the end, Pauly snatched the pigskin and made it across the goal line for a touchdown!

REENIE

Breed(s): border collie mix
Age: 10 weeks
Fun Fact: part-time stand-up comic

They say that border collies love to have a job to do, which makes a dog like Reenie a valuable member of any team. Her biggest job at Puppy Bowl? Looking sooooo cute!

RIVER

Breed(s): Great Pyrenees
Age: 9 weeks
Fun Fact: enjoys long walks on the beach

Big Red may have dominated the last quarter, but River put the shepherd mix in his place in a memorable play. River boldly bounded up and snatched the ball right out of Big Red's paws.

RUDY

Breed(s): basset hound
Age: 17 weeks
Fun Fact: has a smelly sock collection

Basset hounds are known for having a superior sense of smell. Rudy can smell a quarterback sack from a mile away.

SADIE

Breed(s): pit bull
Age: 12 weeks
Fun Fact: sleeps with a teddy bear

Sadie is the quiet, sensitive type, and there's nothing wrong with that. Every team needs a sweetheart!

SAVANNAH

Breed(s): Pomeranian/Maltese mix
Age: 16 weeks
Fun Fact: former disco queen

This fluffy fullback made a splash in the fourth quarter. Savannah believes in saving the best for last.

SHANG

Breed(s): shih tzu
Age: 11 weeks
Fun Fact: practices tackles on the mailman

Shang is the yang to his brother Chih's yin. These brothers normally work together, but sometimes their personalities conflict. In a tail-wagging moment in the third quarter, Shang and Chih struggled for the ball. It was brother versus brother on the thirty-yard line, but in the end Shang was victorious.

SUZIE

Breed(s): basset hound
Age: 17 weeks
Fun Fact: secretly snacks on cat food

Some might say that Suzie is vertically challenged, and that may be true. But her skill stretches all the way across the field.

THELMA

Breed(s): rat terrier/lab/hound mix
Age: 11 weeks
Fun Fact: drives a convertible

Thelma was the first dog out on the field this year, and she quickly captivated fans with her spunky style. This mutt was a real team player.

THIRTEEN

Breed(s): pit bull mix
Age: 12 weeks
Fun Fact: loves to cuddle

After this game, Thirteen might end up with a new nickname: "The Tackler." This pup was not afraid to tumble with the other players if it meant getting his paws on the pigskin.

TWO FACE

Breed(s): boxer mix
Age: 11 weeks
Fun Fact: doesn't need to wear a mask on Halloween

Two Face proved to be one mellow mutt. For a while, he was hanging out on the sidelines with Pauly. Then, this sleepy sweetie got a foul—for Illegal Napping on the Field.

WILLY

Breed(s): heeler mix
Age: 14 weeks
Fun Fact: collects rare coins

Willy ran onto the field in the first quarter, tackling and tumbling at every turn. His high energy was a great start to the game.

A Team of Tail-Gaters

Some of Puppy Bowl's most fur-ocious fans can be found outside the stadium, watching the game from their cars and lounge chairs in the parking lot. They have strong opinions, and they're not afraid to show them by barking, growling, or wagging their tails.

Puppy Bowl fans come in all shapes, sizes, and breeds. Luckily, they all get along, even if they're not rooting for the same side!

This furry fan loves to join in with the cheering crowd.

This puzzled pooch just doesn't understand that last call made by the Ref.

Did You Know?

The first time a football game was combined with a party was probably in 1869 in New Brunswick, New Jersey. Rutgers and Princeton faced off while fans enjoyed food and fun.

On the Sidelines and in the Sky

Puppies aren't the only cute critters to appear in Puppy Bowl. Other adorable animals play important roles in the game by cheering on the players or capturing the action for fans. Let's meet these feathered and furry friends.

Rah, Rah! This cuddly bunny is ready to cheer on her team.

This fluffy fan is on her feet after her favorite player makes a touchdown.

Three Cheers for Chickens!

In Puppy Bowl VII, a newly hatched squad of chicken cheerleaders did an egg-cellent job of rooting for the players.

This happy chicken is shaking his pom-poms for his favorite puppies.

This chicken watches as the game heats up. Maybe he'll do the chicken dance!

Did You Know?

The red fold of skin hanging from a chicken's chin is called a wattle.

High-Flying Hamsters

Once again, a fearless crew of hamsters took control of the blimp to give viewers an aerial look at the field. These chipper critters never slowed down for a moment, making sure to get a great shot every time.

All those buttons might look complicated, but the hamster crew always seems to know exactly what it's doing.

A hamster crew member gets ready for liftoff.

The blimp flew high over the action, giving the hamsters inside the best view in the stadium.

Did You Know?

In the wild, hamsters prefer living underground to being in high places. They can dig tunnels that are three feet deep.

Halftime Highlights

Every major football game needs a spectacular halftime show, and the Puppy Bowl is no different. Every year, the country's cutest kittens get together to entertain fans with their fun feline antics.

So bring on the colored lights . . . the confetti . . . and, of course, the kittens!

Moments before the big show, the kittens backstage practice their moves one last time.

This tabby looks like he's ready for his solo.

Now that's what we call a purr-fect pose! Guess this kitty's ready to face the pup-parazzi.

Can I get a "Meow! Meow!"?

Life in the spotlight isn't for everyone. This kitten looks ready to give up fame and fortune and join the fans.

This gray cutie looks like she's suffering from a confetti overload.

What a face! What fur! This halftime heartthrob might just be the next rock star of the cat world.

What's a halftime show without music? For Puppy Bowl VII, singer John Fulton, host of *Must Love Cats* on Animal Planet™, performed a special tune.

Meet the Ref

An interview with Andrew Schechter, the official Puppy Bowl Referee.

1. When you were a kid, did you dream of becoming a referee for puppies when you grew up?

For as long as I can remember, my dream was to referee puppies pretending to play football in a miniature football stadium. Some children grow up wanting to be school teachers. Others want to be astronauts. I wanted to be a professional puppy referee. And, as you can see, dreams really do come true!

2. How did you get such a cool job?

I like to think I was born into the gig, but, truth be told, I was lucky enough to be in the right place at the right time! As a producer for Animal Planet™, I attended a meeting for Puppy Bowl where we discussed all the details for the big event. When the topic of "talent" arose, I whispered to my boss, "Hey! I can be the Ref!" Knowing I have a background in acting, comedy, and production, my boss suggested me for the "Referee." I have to say, it has been the role of a lifetime!

3. What is the most exciting moment you can remember from a Puppy Bowl game?

There have been many exciting terrier tackles, Fido first downs, and puppy touchdowns, but the most exciting moment each year is when all the puppies get adopted and find loving homes. We're very proud of the fact that all the puppies featured in Puppy Bowl are from shelters and rescue groups, and we're even more proud that we can help provide the puppies a "forever home."

4. How do you keep things under control when the puppies get too frisky?

Well, it's my job to keep a "clean" game in every sense of the word! After blowing the whistle and throwing the yellow flag, I often find myself calling penalties like Unnecessary Ruff-Ruff-Ruffness and Illegal Grasping of the Tail. Nonetheless, every once in a while, there's a puppy player that refuses to listen! Even to the Ref! Can you believe that? Luckily, there are more Excessive Cuteness fouls than anything else!

5. Did you ever get splashed by a puppy at the water bowl?

Yes! In Puppy Bowl VII, right after I called an Illegal Use of the Paws penalty on a Pyrenees puppy, he jumped into the water bowl and began splashing me with his hind legs. I guess he wasn't too happy with the call! I was soaked, but I'm glad he had a chance to "voice" his opinion while practicing the doggy paddle.

6. What advice would you give to the puppy players in the next Puppy Bowl?

Keep your paws to yourself and no "trash" barking! And if you see a chew toy, carry it over the goal line to score a puppy touchdown! Who knows, with enough big plays, you could be next year's MVP (that's Most Valuable *Puppy*, of course)!

7. Is there one puppy in particular that stands out from all the Puppy Bowls you've been in?

All the puppies have been so adorable and rambunctious that it's difficult to choose just one from the group. I do, however, specifically remember one corgi puppy that decided to steal the yellow flag from my back pocket. Suddenly, I was part of the action, chasing the puppy up and down the field to retrieve my flag. I definitely called an Unpuppylike Conduct penalty on that troublemaker!

8. Do you have any pets?

It may be hard to believe, but I do not have any pets. In fact, I do not think any animal would be too happy living in my closet-sized New York City apartment!

9. If you were a dog, what breed would you be?

I would have to be a dalmatian. We both "wear" black and white!

10. What is the most important quality a Puppy Bowl Ref needs to have?

A Puppy Bowl Ref needs to have thick skin (for puppy nibbling), a sense of humor (you can't take this job too seriously!), and a big heart (spending a day with over forty puppies will make anyone's heart melt). And you can't be afraid to get between a slobbery kiss and some puppy breath—it happens all too often!

Speak Like the Ref

Want to play along with the Ref during Puppy Bowl?
Then you'll need to know how to make the tough calls.

Excessive Barking

A yip or a yap here and there is allowed, but when a pup can't stop barking, it's time to call a foul.

Excessive Cuteness

All puppies are cute, but when they purposely turn on the extra charm, it can be distracting to the other players—not to mention the fans.

Illegal Defense, Goaltending

Plopping down in front of the goalposts might fly in a soccer game, but in Puppy Bowl it's against the rules.

Illegal Grasping of the Tail

A wagging tail is hard for another puppy to resist, but chomping down on another player's tail is a no-no in this game.

Illegal Napping on the Field

All puppies need their sleep, but not when it interferes with the game.

Illegal Use of the Paws

A player can use his or her paws to run across the field, splash in the water bowl, or grab the ball—but not to pummel another puppy.

Intentional Grounding

Tackling is allowed, but at some point, you just have to let go!

Puppy Hydration Break

It's the Ref's job to keep an eye on the water bowl. When it's empty, he blows the whistle and refills it, making sure every thirsty pup gets a chance to drink.

Puppy Substitution

When a player poops out or fouls out, the Ref can call in another player to replace him or her.

Puppy Touchdown

If a puppy has the ball in her paws and crosses the goal line in either end zone, it's a touchdown! Technically, only the ball has to cross the line as long as the pup has it in her possession.

Pup to Pup Coverage

This term describes when one puppy sticks close to another puppy to make sure his opponent doesn't get the ball and score.

Splashing on the Field

Every pup needs a water break, but some players just get silly and start splashing water everywhere—and that's a foul.

Unnecessary Ruff-Ruff-Ruffness

Scuffles on the field happen all the time, but the Ref has to make sure nobody gets hurt. Puppies who don't know when to stop get charged with this foul.

Puppy Bowl Time Line

Every year Puppy Bowl fans are treated to a new team of puppies and tons of new surprises. In this section you'll see photos of some of the most memorable moments from the last seven years—from jaw-dropping plays to extreme incidents of cuteness.

Puppy Bowl I, 2005

When the first Puppy Bowl aired, fans weren't sure what to expect. But they were quickly captivated by the pups frolicking on the field. Everybody wanted more Puppy Bowl!

Puppy Bowl II, 2006

In the second round, fourteen players took to the field, and the first-ever kitty halftime show was added.

Puppy Bowl III, 2007

With Puppy Bowl more popular than ever, the official tail-gaters swarmed to the stadium to turn this puppy playoff into a real party.

Puppy Bowl IV, 2008

Referee Andrew Schechter appeared on the field for the first time, quickly becoming a fan favorite.

Puppy Bowl V, 2009

With fans clamoring for more views of the game, the hamster pilots took to the air to get shots from above.

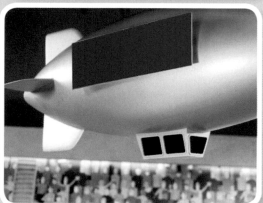

Puppy Bowl VI, 2010

Every player needs to be cheered on and, in this Puppy Bowl, fluffy bunnies waved their pom-poms on the sidelines.

Puppy Bowl VII, 2011

Chicken cheerleaders replaced the bunnies, and doggy movie stars from Disney Studios paid a special visit.

Highlights: Puppy Bowl VII

CB
the shih tzu/beagle mix

MVP
Puppy Bowl VII

He wasn't the biggest or the strongest on the field, but doggone it, this puppy was the fastest on four legs. Fans couldn't keep up with this furry ball of fire. CB played his heart out on both offense and defense, earning him the game's highest honor.

Big Red Scores!

Early in the first quarter, Big Red got control of the ball and raced for the end zone . . . and then fumbled! But this shepherd mix wasn't about to disappoint his furry fans. He recovered the ball and bounded to the goal line to make the first touchdown of the game.

Awwwww!

Who says cuteness is a crime? The Puppy Bowl Ref, that's who. He gave adorable River a foul for Excessive Cuteness! That's River on the right with his brother Oliver—a double dose of cuteness.

Taking It Easy

Thirteen took a time-out from tackling his teammates to chill out on the fence. Even a star player needs a break now and then.

No Ruff Stuff!

When there's a puppy scuffle on the field, the Ref steps in to gently break things up.

Photo Finish

Spunky Calvin had two close calls in the second quarter. After stealing the ball from Booda, he ran for a touchdown—but did he make it? A review of the play showed that Calvin missed scoring by just a few inches. But Calvin recovered quickly, grabbing the ball from CB. He ran for the end zone and got the ball just over the goal line to make the touchdown.

Let Me Think About It . . .

The fans went wild when Reenie got control of the ball just steps away from the red zone. But instead of grabbing the ball and going for a touchdown, Reenie kept it in her sights. A staring contest with a football? That's a Puppy Bowl first!

A Puppy-Side View

Puppy Bowl VII brought another first to the legacy of this great game: the Puppy Cam. Fans finally got to see what the game looked like from the point of view of the players. Here, Pauly sports the special camera.

Fido Face-Off

Sweet-faced shepherd mix Jessie came alive in the fourth quarter. Shortly after committing a foul by boldly stealing the flag, she gained control of the ball. That's when Jack jumped in and took the ball right from under her paws! Then he sped off to score the game's last touchdown.

Highlights:
Puppy Bowl VI

JAKE
the Chihuahua/pug mix

MVP
Puppy Bowl VI

Like CB, Puppy Bowl VII's MVP, Jake was selected for the game's biggest honor for his speedy moves on the field. Right out of the gate, he began racing back and forth across the field, running circles around the defense. He didn't slow down until the game was over.

Two Brawling Boys

In the first quarter, Rigley, a French bulldog, went head-to-head with Jersey Boy, a Yorkie mix. The Ref had to break up the scuffle and fouled them both for Unnecessary Ruff-Ruff-Ruffness.

A Splash-tacular Touchdown

Chloe the lab mix was a pup to watch right from the start. First, she sparred with husky mix Bandit over possession of the ball, making an exciting interception that got the fans howling. Then she fumbled the ball in the end zone but recovered it quickly and ran through the water bowl to make a touchdown! She's one pup who knows how to make a big splash on the field.

Loving Care

Before the game, Dr. Elisa Mazzaferro of the American Animal Hospital Association (AAHA) checked the puppies to make sure they were in good shape to play. Here, she gives Yorkie mix Addison a clean bill of health.

A Furry Fava-rite

Feisty Fava, a cattle dog mix, started the game with a high-flying jump, soaring over two puppies! A few minutes later, she followed up with the first puppy touchdown, breezing into the end zone. But Fava wasn't finished. She raced across the field to make a second touchdown on the other side.

Twin Tacklers

It was the third quarter, and French bulldog Yums had the ball on the forty-yard line. Then brothers Toby and Tigger, two collie mixes, joined forces and bulldozed Yums with a tackle that knocked her off her paws. Those twins are double trouble!

A Close Call

Fans went wild in the third quarter when Dixon, a shepherd mix, scored a touchdown. Or did he? The play was challenged, and the crowd waited patiently as the Ref reviewed the play. The call on the field stood, and Dixon was one pleased puppy.

Bunny Boosters

Puppy Bowl VI was the first year cheerleaders joined the game—but these cheerleaders weren't the egg-laying kind. Instead, adorable, fluffy bunnies rooted for their favorite players by twitching their whiskers and wiggling their ears.

A Meeting of the Mutts

These pups got together during the game to figure out their next move.

Highlights: Puppy Bowl V

MATILDA
the beagle mix

MVP
Puppy Bowl V

Matilda's magic moment happened late in the second quarter when she ran all the way down the field for a touchdown. Before the fans had stopped clapping, Matilda had made another score. And then another! No player in Puppy Bowl history had ever made so many touchdowns in a single play.

A Dynamic Duo

As soon as the game began, Elvira, a Catahoula mix (right), and Eli the Aussie shepherd (left) sprang into action. Eli made a tackle at the twenty-yard line, and then moments later Elvira tackled Eli, grabbed the ball, and ran for a touchdown.

Oh, Say Can You Squawk . . .

At the start of the game, Pepper the Parrot screeched out the national anthem for the standing crowd.

Bella Breaks Away

In the first quarter, Bella the bull terrier was covered by Sugar, a white Chihuahua half her size. Bella finally lost Sugar's tail and went after the ball.

That Moose Can Move!

Moose, a shaggy Australian shepherd, stunned the crowd with a spectacular run for the end zone in the first half. He whizzed across the goal line for the touchdown.

Confetti Cover-Up

This cute kitty performer almost got lost in mountains of confetti during the halftime show, but luckily she didn't get swept up by the cleaning crew.

Furry Face-Off

Buster the hound mix might look like a bruiser, but Ocee, a Pekingnese, wasn't afraid to face him on the field.

Nap Time!

Husky/shepherd mix Schroeder was frisky when he first got on the field, but by the third quarter, this tyke was tuckered out. Schroeder used the football as a pillow and slept for the rest of the game.

Look, Ma, No Fur!

After halftime, things heated up on the field when the Ref scooped up a streaker dashing across the arena. It turns out that the troublemaker was just a Chinese crested, a mostly hairless breed of dog.

Highlights: Puppy Bowl IV

ABIGAIL
the Jack Russell terrier

MVP
Puppy Bowl IV

This superpup came flying off the bench ready to rumble. She stole the ball at the thirty-yard line and then began racing up and down the field. The entire defensive line chased her, but she was unstoppable. Running laps around the competition earned her the game's highest award.

Jackson's Double Touchdown

Jackson, one of the greatest wide receivers in Puppy Bowl history, sped down the end zone to score a touchdown. Abigail knocked the ball out of his paws, but he recovered and scored again.

Two Fluffy Fireballs

For most of the game, these two fuzzy pups were nothing but a blur on the field. Finnegan, a Cavachon, and Elle, a Havanese, tousled throughout all four quarters, putting on a great show for the fans.

A Bold, Little Beagle

Bruin, an Alaskan malamute, was the biggest puppy on the field. But that didn't stop Attucker, a beagle, from facing this gentle giant. He went right after the big guy, making sure Bruin didn't dominate the game.

Furry Face-Off

The crowd got quiet as Bingo, Daisy's brother, and Jack, a lab mix, carefully considered each other. Which player would make the first move?

Ready for My Close-Up

Golden retriever Dixie checked out the cameras as soon as she ran onto the field.

The Nose Knows

The puppies took a break from the action to sniff out the competition. That's one smelly strategy!

Guarding the Goal

It looks like Justin, a Westie, got confused and thought he was at a hockey game. He's lucky he didn't get a foul for Illegal Goaltending!

Tiny Tough Guy

Tucker, the smallest puppy on the field, got a foul for holding on to Bailey, a King Charles/Havanese mix. But the Ref's warning didn't have much of an impact on him—he went after Jackson, a Westie, next. The Ref had no choice but to eject him from the game.

Kimmi's True Colors

On the forty-yard line, Kimmi, a beagle, tackled Raven, a beagle/mini pinscher mix. But Kimmi wouldn't let go, and the Ref called her out for Illegal Holding.

Highlights:
Puppy Bowl III

Porsche vs. the Puggle

Porsche, a boxer, and Sonny, a puggle, spent the first half of the game brawling. Their rivalry was fun for the fans, who enjoyed the nonstop action.

Lucy's Revenge

Lucy, a shepherd mix, may look like a sweetheart, but don't mess with her! Checkers, a lab, learned that lesson the hard way. After he sacked Lucy in the first half, she got back at him by nipping him. That bite got her ejected from the game.

Three Brothers

Buffy, Bomber, and Buster were three brothers who could have teamed together to dominate the game. Instead, these Samoyed cuties spent more time playing with one another and hanging out by the goal.

Ascot's Amazing Run

Ascot, a cocker spaniel/dachshund mix, impressed everyone with a fifty-yard run in the first half of the game. Bess did her best to stop this speedy pup, but despite her dogged pursuit, Ascot got the yardage, making him the game's leading rusher.

Hello, Larry!

Larry, a vizsla, took a break from the game to check out the view from the guardrail. The fans were happy to have Larry's undivided attention.

A Standoff

Things got tense when these puppies surrounded the game balls, eyeing one another. The fans watched breathlessly, wondering who would make the first move.

A Rescued Success

One of the star players of the game was Tabasco, a mixed-breed dog rescued after Hurricane Katrina hit New Orleans. This Cajun cutie made many exciting plays, including this tackle of Questor.

Highlights: Puppy Bowl II

Barry the Poodle

Poodles are known for being smart, and Barry proved they're also bold. Within the first two minutes of the game, he bravely busted into the end zone. Go Barry!

Fierce and Fluffy

This fluffy player seemed to send a message to his opponents with just one look: Don't mess with me!

Tug-of-War

When two pups go after the same ball, watch out! Things can get fierce until one pup gives up—or gets bored and goes to play in the water bowl.

Mine, All Mine!

Any chew toy on the field is considered in play and can be used to make a touchdown. Most of the time, though, pups like this Australian cattle dog would rather hang out and chew than carry the ball across the goal line.

Put Me In, Coach!

Some dogs jump right into the action without waiting, while others, like these two cute puppies, seem to need further instruction.

Nose to Nose

It's not unusual for dogs to face off on the field, but this water bowl showdown was a Puppy Bowl first. The big pup has an edge on the smaller competitor—but in the end, it comes down to the thirstiest dog.

Highlights:
Puppy Bowl I

Bandit the Terrier

Bandit made the greatest comeback in Puppy Bowl history. As the play clock ran down in the fourth quarter, Bandit took on three pups all at once. For his bravery, Bandit earned Puppy Bowl's first-ever Most Valuable Puppy award.

How Do We Look?

These two picture-perfect pups were eager to get on camera.

Pup to Pup Coverage

Even though this was Puppy Bowl's first year, players quickly learned the art of defense.

Time for a Chew Break

While the art of defense came naturally to the players, it took some time for the pups to figure out they needed to get the ball across the goal line. Most of the time, they chilled out with chew toys.

Back Off, Big Guys!

Roxi, a spunky corgi mix, was one of the smallest players on the field, but she didn't let any of the big guys grab her favorite chew toy.

Bowl Cam Debuts

The water bowl cam has been around since the very first Puppy Bowl. Here, French bulldog Itsy takes a drink.

Chew on This

Before each Puppy Bowl begins, producers must gather the equipment the pups will need to play. They need fresh water for the water bowl, the Ref's whistle, and something to clean up any "accidents" on the field. But most importantly, the field needs to be stocked with plenty of chew toys for the energetic pups. Here are some of the players' all-time favorites.

Bones

What dog doesn't love a bone? On the field, you'll see bones of all types. Some are fluffy and plush, while others are made of vinyl (and might even squeak).

Braided Rope

You can't get more basic than a braided length of rope. Puppies will often use them to play tug-of-war with other pups.

Cute Critters

Outside, the site of a furry rodent scurrying around will get any pup's tail wagging. That's probably why the players love this stuffed chipmunk toy.

Footballs

What football game would be complete without an actual football? In Puppy Bowl, of course, the footballs are anything but ordinary. There are furry footballs, fuzzy footballs, vinyl footballs, footballs with a rope dangling from either end, and even footballs with arms and legs!

Long "Loofah" Dogs

These stuffed dogs, with their long, skinny bodies and short legs, are modeled after dachshunds. They're the perfect shape for the pups to pick up and carry across the goal for a touchdown.

The Ref

When puppies disagree with the Ref's calls, they can take out their frustration by chewing on a stuffed referee toy.

Round Balls

While footballs might be the most popular, the pups also enjoy tennis balls, colorful balls, squeaky balls, and other kinds of balls.

Puppy Bowl Party Time!

Most pups are happiest in packs, and you will be, too, if you invite some friends over to watch Puppy Bowl with you. Here are some ideas that will make your party guests sit up and pay attention.

Invitations

E-mail invitations are just fine, but you can make handmade ones that will really get your guests excited. With a parent's help, cut a simple bone shape out of construction paper or cardstock, and write all of your party's information on one side.

PUPPY BOWL PARTY!
COME TO OUR PUPPY BOWL PARTY!
Where: Our House
When: 1 PM
Who: Dogs and Humans Welcome!

Decorations

🐾 Show your guests where to go by drawing paw prints in chalk that lead right to your door.

🐾 Give a white paper tablecloth a doggy touch. Cut a circle out of a kitchen sponge, about two inches in diameter. Dab the sponge onto a black ink pad and stamp circles all over for a dalmatian look, or group the circles together to make paw prints. You could also do this with paper place mats instead.

🐾 Use the bone pattern you used for your invitation to make a paper decoration you can hang over a window, a door, or across a wall. Cut out lots of paper bones, then use a hole punch to punch a hole in each end. Then attach two bones together with yarn. For a simpler way to do it, attach the bones at each end with a stapler.

🐾 Serve snacks in colorful (new) plastic dog bowls. Jazz them up with designs made with tubes of glitter paint.

Games

🐾 **Pin the Tail on the Puppy**: Get a poster of a dog or draw a picture of a dog on a large piece of poster board and hang it on an empty spot on your wall. Then make tails out of cardstock paper and write each of your guests' names on a tail. Put a loop of tape on the back of each tail. Blindfold each guest, spin them around, and instruct them to pin their tail on the puppy. The guest with the tail closest to the right spot is the winner.

🐾 **Puppy Trainer Says**: This is just like Simon Says, but the puppy trainer tells the players to do different dog tricks. The trainer always starts with "Puppy trainer says" and adds the trick, like "Puppy trainer says sit" or "Puppy trainer says roll over." If the puppy trainer doesn't say "puppy trainer" before the trick, and players do the trick, anyway, they are out of the game. The winner is the player who outlasts all the others.

🐾 **Doggie Dance Party**: Get an adult to help you load your MP3 player with dog-themed songs like: "Who Let the Dogs Out" by Baha Men, "Walking the Dog" by Rufus Thomas, "Quiche Lorraine" by The B-52's, "Diamond Dogs" by David Bowie, and "Gonna Buy Me a Dog" by The Monkees. Have fun dancing with your friends, or take it a step further by awarding prizes for the best doggy-inspired dance moves.

Food for People

What's the best food to serve at a Puppy Bowl party? Hot dogs, of course! Make them special by wrapping each hot dog in a "blanket"—one triangle-shaped crescent roll from a can. Put the dogs on a cookie sheet, and have an adult bake them at 350 degrees Fahrenheit for about twenty minutes, until the rolls are nicely browned.

Decorate cupcakes to look like puppies. Make your favorite cupcake mix and ice with white or chocolate frosting. Use round, candy-coated chocolates for eyes. A red or pink jelly bean makes a cute nose. Break a round, chocolate cookie wafer in half to make two ears. Then draw on a mouth with black or red writing gel and add a pink or red jelly bean tongue.

Doggy Bags

Who doesn't love getting a gift bag at the end of a party? Since this is a Puppy Bowl party, give your guests doggy bags instead. You can include treats for them as well as their pets:

- dog bone–shaped cookie cutters
- dog stickers or rubber stamps
- a small dog toy, such as a tennis ball
- a catnip mouse for kitty friends who couldn't come to the party

Food for Puppies

Many websites have great recipes for homemade dog treats that are safe for puppies to eat. Here is a simple recipe for tasty peanut butter biscuits that your furry guests are sure to love.

Peanut Butter Biscuits

2 cups whole wheat flour

1 tablespoon baking powder

1 cup natural peanut butter (the natural kind is important, because regular peanut butter has additives that aren't good for dogs)

1/2 cup skim milk

1/2 cup plain, nonfat yogurt

1. Preheat the oven to 375 degrees Fahrenheit.
2. Mix the flour and baking powder together in a large bowl.
3. In another bowl, mix together the peanut butter, skim milk, and yogurt. Then add that to the dry ingredients.
4. Mix together until everything is blended. Then put your ball of dough on a floured surface and knead.
5. Use a rolling pin to roll out the dough until it's about 1/2 inch thick.
6. Cut out shapes with a bone-shaped cookie cutter (or use any shape you like).
7. Put the biscuits on a baking sheet covered with parchment paper and bake for twenty minutes, until lightly browned.
8. Cool them on a rack before giving them to your guests. They should be stored in an airtight container.

Adopt Your Own Furry Friend

If your family is thinking about adopting a puppy, you can visit these websites for more information. Learn what it takes to care for a dog and find dogs in your area that are available for adoption.

Where to Start

Petfinder

www.petfinder.com

Need help locating a pet for adoption in your neighborhood? Try Petfinder's zip code search to see what kinds of pets are looking for a new home or to find a local animal shelter.

The American Society for the Prevention of Cruelty to Animals (ASPCA)

www.aspca.org

This site has information about pet adoption to get you started, including articles on pet care and finding the right animal for your family.

American Humane Association (AHA)

www.americanhumane.org

This site will help you decide if you're ready to adopt a pet and learn more about the adoption process.

The Humane Society of the United States (HSUS)

www.humanesociety.org

Check out this site to find articles about choosing a pet, shelter adoption, and more.

Friends of Puppy Bowl

**These organizations provided the puppies for Puppy Bowl VII.
Unless otherwise noted, they can be found by searching** *www.petfinder.com*.

All Star Pet Rescue
American Fox Terrier Rescue
Annapolis Dog Rescue
Appalachian Great Pyrenees Rescue (agorescue.com)
Blue Earth Nicollet County Humane Society (benchs.org)
Bonnie's Animal Rescue Kingdom
Butch's Place Animal Rescue
Catawba County Animal Services
Crossing Paths Animal Rescue
Georgia Animal Rescue and Defence Inc.
Happy Endings Dog Rescue
Humane Society of Richland County
Island Dog Inc.
Katzenwoofers Pet Rescue
Kids to the Rescue
Luvfurmutts Animal Rescue
Mid-Atlantic Basset Hound Rescue
Mini Aussie Rescue and Support
Mini Mutts Rescue
Oldies but Goodies Cocker Spaniel Rescue
Pet Assistance League of Virginia
Posey Shelter Pet Promoters Inc.
Save the Orphaned Pets, Inc.
Sittin' Pretty
Underdogs
Unleashed

Kittens provided by:
Pennsylvania SPCA

Chickens provided by:
Maranatha Farm's Animal Sanctuary